The Nutcracker

By Rita Balducci
Illustrated by Sheilah Beckett

A GOLDEN BOOK • NEW YORK

Text copyright © 1991, 2014 by Random House LLC. Illustrations copyright © 2014 by Sheilah Beckett. All rights reserved. Published in the United States by Golden Books, an imprint of Random House Children's Books, a division of Random House LLC, a Penguin Random House Company, 1745 Broadway, New York, NY 10019. Golden Books, A Golden Book, A Little Golden Book, the G colophon, and the distinctive gold spine are registered trademarks of Random House LLC.
Visit us on the Web!
randomhouse.com/kids
Educators and librarians, for a variety of teaching tools, visit us at
RHTeachersLibrarians.com
Library of Congress Control Number: 2013946781
ISBN 978-0-385-36993-0
Printed in the United States of America
10 9 8 7 6 5 4 3 2 1

Once there was a little girl named Clara whose family was having a wonderful party on a snowy Christmas Eve.

"Merry Christmas!" she said as she greeted each guest.

The last guest to arrive was Clara's godfather, Herr Drosselmeyer. All the children loved him very much because he was a toymaker and a wonderful storyteller. Clara thought he could even perform magic!

"Merry Christmas, Clara," he said, presenting her with a heavy package.

"Merry Christmas—and thank you!" Clara
cried, lifting a large wooden nutcracker from the
wrappings. "He looks like a very brave soldier,"
she said.

"And so he is," Herr Drosselmeyer replied.

Just then the musicians began to play
a lively tune, and all the grown-ups began
to dance.

Clara carried her nutcracker over to where her cousins and friends were all playing with their new toys. Holding him carefully, she softly hummed a Christmas carol. All of a sudden Clara's little brother, Fritz, jumped up from behind her chair and grabbed the nutcracker.

"No, Fritz, no!" Clara cried, chasing him.
Soon all the children were running after Fritz.
But the nutcracker was very heavy, and Fritz was
a very little boy. The nutcracker crashed to the
floor and broke.

Clara sadly picked up her injured nutcracker
and showed him to Herr Drosselmeyer.

"Why, Clara," he said, tying his handkerchief around the nutcracker's broken jaw, "many good soldiers get hurt in battle. This will be his bandage, and you will be his nurse." And he wiped her tears away and handed the nutcracker back to her.

Clara was a good little nurse. She gently tucked the nutcracker into the doll's bed she had received as a Christmas present. She stayed by his side until all the guests had gone home. Then she kissed him good night and went up to bed.

But Clara could not stop thinking about her nutcracker. So back downstairs she crept, and lifted him from the little bed. Then she curled up on the sofa and fell asleep with the nutcracker in her arms.

While Clara was sleeping, Herr Drosselmeyer came into the room. He quietly took the handkerchief off the nutcracker's jaw and gently waved it over Clara and her new toy. Suddenly the nutcracker was transformed into a handsome prince, standing guard over Clara while she slept.

Later that night Clara woke up. The house, the tree, and the toys seemed to be getting larger. Tremendous mice were running all over the room. Then she saw the prince bravely battling a mouse wearing a crown.

"Leave him alone!" Clara shouted at the wicked mice. She jumped off the sofa and threw her slipper at the Mouse King, hitting him squarely on the head. He fell to the floor, and the other mice ran off, carrying their leader.

"Thank you for your help, Clara," said the prince, picking up the crown that had fallen from the Mouse King's head. "I would like to invite you to the Land of Sweets to meet the Sugar Plum Fairy, who is ruling there until I return."

The prince placed the crown upon Clara's head, and her nightgown changed into a beautiful shimmering dress.

and Russian dancers did a splendid candy-cane dance, jumping high into the air!

At the end of the evening, the Sugar Plum
Fairy twirled gracefully with her cavalier. Clara
sighed as she watched the beautiful dance.

"Now we must depart," the prince told Clara. "But one day we will return to the Land of Sweets."

As the two rode off in their magical sleigh, Clara felt that she was in a beautiful dream . . . of a Christmas Eve she would never forget.